W9-ALE-025

Drum City

by **Thea Guidone**

Illustrations by **Vanessa Newton**

TRICYCLE PRESS
Berkeley

Drum.
Drum.

Boy in the yard
drumming so **hard,**

calling all kids
to come drum in the yard.

Drum on some kettles and cans!

Here they come!

They run to the beat of the **drum.**

Drum.

Bowls and
buckets,
cartons
and cans,
barrels
and bins,
and pots
and pans,

mops on pails,

and **rusty** old rails—

a frolicking, rollicking ruckus of rumbling **drums**.

Drum.

Jump to the sound,
dance all around,

loud on the tubs and the
tins that they found.

"March!" calls the boy
in the yard full of drums,

hundreds and
hundreds of
drums.

Hum of the city.

Humdrum of the city. **Ho**-hum.

Something is coming.

> They watch and they wonder,

assuming the booming

> is summertime thunder.

Thumping and **pounding,**

> the echo resounding

the sound of the

> pound of the **drums.**

Drum.

Buses and cabs,

bakers and cops,

people in **banks**,

people in shops,

everywhere, everything, everyone

STOPS

for **kids** marching in with their **drums.**

Drum.

People in traffic keeping the beat
on the **hood** and the trunk
and the bicycle seat.

Mamas in rollers
rock babies in strollers,

clapping and **stomp**ing and
stamping their feet to the

drums.

Drum.

Drums everywhere,
in the park, in the square,

by the pond with the ducks,
in the zoo with the bear.

From Hill Street to Main
to Sassafras Lane,

kids shake up
the city with

drums.

Drum.

The **city** becomes a city of **drums**,
banging and clanging as **everyone** comes.

A **summer** parade, a drummer parade,
a magical bucket-and-bowl
serenade

Drum.

Up in the **planes**,
down at the docks,

bang on a lid or a crate
or a **box**.

Everyone jams.
Everyone
rocks.

Everyone,
beat on your
drum.

Drum.

Play **hard**, play soft,
　　　play happy or **blue**.

You listen to **me**.
　　　I listen to **you**.

Over the mountains
and over the **sea**,

drumming like you,
drumming like me.

Together we **drum**.

Let's

drum!

For kids in my family and kids in "The Group."
—T.G.

This is dedicated to my sister, my friend,
my 20/20 and my hilariously funny family.
Thank you JC, Ray, Coy, Will, Zoe, Ben, Chyna,
The Jeans, Loredan, Ms. I, and Dad.
Love y'all.
—V.N.

Copyright © 2010 by Thea Guidone
Illustrations copyright © 2010 by Vanessa Newton

All rights reserved. Published in the United States by Tricycle Press, an imprint of the
Crown Publishing Group, a division of Random House, Inc., New York.
www.crownpublishing.com
www.tricyclepress.com

Tricycle Press and the Tricycle Press colophon are registered trademarks of Random House, Inc.

Library of Congress Cataloging-in-Publication Data
Guidone, Thea.
Drum city / by Thea Guidone; illustrations by Vanessa Newton. — 1st ed.
p. cm.
Summary: A young boy begins banging on pots and pans in his front yard, enticing
other children to join him, and before long the entirecity is feeling the beat.
[1. Stories in rhyme. 2. Drum—Fiction.] I. Newton, Vanessa, ill. II.
Title.
PZ8.3.G948Dru 2010
[E]—dc22
2009031747

ISBN 978-1-58246-308-7 (hardcover) — ISBN 978-1-58246-348-3 (Gibraltar lib. bdg.)

Printed in China

Design by Becky James

Typeset in CheapSignage. The illustrations in this book were rendered in Photoshop.

1 2 3 4 5 6 — 14 13 12 11 10

First Edition